Sugar's Cookies

VEE TAYLOR

Copyright © 2024 by Vee Taylor

All rights reserved. No part of this book may be used or reproduced in any form whatsoever without written permission except in the case of brief quotations in critical articles or reviews.

This book is a work of fiction. Names, characters, businesses, organizations, places, events and incidents either are the product of the author's imagination or are used fictitiously. Any resemblance to actual persons, living or dead, events, or locales is entirely coincidental.

http://www.veetaylorauthor.com

Cover design by The Sparrow Collective

Editing by Indie Edits with Jeanine

Proofing by Celena Santana

First Edition: December 2024

 Created with Vellum

Author's Note

There are no characters in this book based off anyone, it is just part of my imagination.
There are also organizations that don't exist in today's world, so because this is a work of fiction, we can safely also assume that these are stretched to fit our imagination.

This book is all about pure enjoyment—spice-forward with cringey, unfiltered elements. After writing some really angsty and emotional novels lately, I wanted to toss this little novella into the mix for fun.
I want to emphasize that every body is amazing and beautiful. Sugar has a unique kink that isn't meant to hurt or shame any body type because in this space, we embrace and celebrate every shape, size, and form. This novella is intentionally spicy, unfiltered, and lighthearted, serving as a playful palette cleanser between my more intense, angsty reads.
This book contains: lactation play, breeding play, quirky names for the male anatomy, death of a parent (in the past), small male genitalia play, and 'good boy' play.

Dedication

To my late grandmother who once asked me how big my boyfriend's peen was in the middle of a family dinner.

Sugar

Moving to a small town surrounded by cornfields in central Illinois was never something I'd planned. But when I stumbled across an ad for a bakery-ready commercial space in Rantucky, Illinois, it felt like a sign. So, I packed my bags, quit my corporate job, and left the big city behind.

What I didn't expect was for the town to look like it had been ripped straight out of a Hallmark movie. Main Street was lined with adorable little brick buildings, each one boasting a quirky, hand-painted sign practically begging you to come in. Flower baskets hung from the streetlamps, and little boutiques were on every corner. It was like this place was in a contest for "Most Charming Town Ever," and it was crushing the competition. The whole place gave off that "everyone knows everyone" small-town energy, and I half expected someone to stroll up and offer me a pie —then I remembered that I was supposed to be the one baking the pies now.

In the sea of vintage pickup trucks, my bright, shiny sports car stuck out like a sore thumb. I could practically feel their side-eye, like "Who let the city slicker in?" But instead of feeling out of place, I couldn't help but grin. This town, with its friendly faces and molasses-slow pace, might just be the perfect place for my new chapter.

I sighed as I pulled up to the little bakery on the corner. According to the ad, it was fully equipped and ready to go. The former owners had retired to some tropical paradise, leaving me to live out my *Great British Bake Off* dreams. The only hiccup? I had no idea how to bake. Like, at all. But hey, details, right?

When I told my best friend, Tammie, about this genius plan, she nearly fell off her chair from laughing so hard. "You're moving to the middle of cornfields to open a bakery? You? The woman who once set off the smoke alarm making toast?"

Yeah, okay, so maybe it was a little wild. But who cares? Fresh starts are supposed to be a little wild.

I grabbed my phone and hit video call.

It only took two rings before Tammie's grinning face appeared, her wild red hair all over the place. "Well, if it isn't Betty Crocker herself," she teased.

"Ha. Ha."

"You know I'm just teasing you, Sugar."

"Look," I squealed. "There she is."

I turned the camera around and pointed to a wooden storefront in the middle of the small downtown.

"I cannot believe it." Tammie's mouth dropped open in shock. "Have you been looking at recipes lately?"

Ever since I found out I was moving here, I'd been attempting, without much success, to learn how to bake. Cookies were about the only thing I could manage to make somewhat right—everything else either ended up burnt or barely cooked.

"Yeah," I said while flipping the camera back toward me.

"Any luck?" Tammie asked, already bracing herself.

She'd been the unfortunate guinea pig for my many *culinary disasters*. Let's just say she still hadn't fully recovered from the "charred brownies" incident.

"I'm getting there." I shrugged, trying to sound casual.

My parents named me Sugar because my mom had an intense sweet tooth while pregnant. It was meant to be ironic, but I thought it was the worst name, well, at least until I decided to open a bakery. I wished they'd gotten to see this. It would have been their dream to be here, too. They died in a kitchen fire when I was just a baby, all thanks to a batch of sugar cookies my mom was baking for their restaurant. And, of course, kids at school had a field day with that one. "Oh, Sugar, you're the reason your parents died—killed by sugar!"

Tammie sighed dramatically, and even over a video call, I could feel her judgment. "You know you can come home," she began, her voice taking on that soft, coaxing tone that always made me feel like I was five years old, not a grown woman dealing with her own complicated life. "You've always been so hard on yourself, always thinking that every mistake is a sign that you're doomed to be alone forever. But that's just not true. There's more to life than finding the perfect person, and you're allowed to take a step back, you're allowed to be imperfect, and you're allowed to have a reset when things don't work out."

She paused, letting her words sink in, but not for too long. Tammie never really gave me time to react before launching into her next monologue. "I mean, look at me. You think I have it all figured out? Absolutely not. But you have to give yourself a chance to be happy, and sometimes that means accepting the fact that you're not going to find someone who ticks every box. Maybe, just maybe, there's a guy out there who's been through his own rough patches, his own messes, and he's not going to judge you for yours. You deserve that, you know? You deserve to let someone see the real you—even the parts that aren't perfect."

I sat there, speechless, swallowing the lump in my throat as she finally paused, letting out a breath.

"Stop hiding behind this idea that you have to be flawless or that every failure means you're destined to be alone. It's okay to come home, take a break, and let yourself believe that there's someone out there who'll love you exactly the way you are."

Her words hung in the air, heavy and honest, and for once, I didn't have a snappy retort ready.

"It's not because of Rick," I huffed.

And it wasn't. Rick and I lasted a whole month before I called it quits. He was just like Rob, James, Bob, and John—perfectly fine, perfectly bland.

"I just think you have high expectations," Tammie went on. "You're waiting for the perfect man, and, honey, that guy doesn't exist."

"My expectations aren't *that* ridiculous," I shot back, rolling my eyes.

They weren't . . . I swear.

"You complained about one thing," Tammie started. "They all had big—"

"I'm in public," I whisper-yelled into the phone, showing off my marvelous chins. "Shut up."

Tammie rolled her eyes as I pulled the phone away from me. "—Beaver Bashers."

"Beaver Basher?" I giggled and quickly covered my mouth.

"You know what I mean," Tammie said.

"There is nothing wrong with wanting one that is petite and fits nicely."

All my exes were fine, and to be honest, I thought Rick might've been the one. But the moment he dropped his pants and revealed his Ankle Spanker, I knew it was over. I was so tired of these guys with their giant Ham Candles. Seriously, was it too much to ask for something small and manageable?

Big dicks were just . . . terrifying. They never got me off, and I was a hole for their pleasure. When Rick would leave my house, I'd find myself scrolling through videos of tiny dicks afterward, just to get off. It wasn't that the big ones hurt; they were just . . . not my vibe. I fantasized about a soft little joystick, one I could coax to life in my mouth.

Honestly, I think it all started with my childhood obsession with those Hatch-a-Dinosaur toys—you know, the ones that grew in water? Maybe that translated into my kink for tiny dicks. I wanted something I could actually wrap my tongue around without feeling like I was trying to deepthroat a kielbasa. I wanted to handle it all, comfortably, without the fear of being stuffed like a Thanksgiving turkey.

I threw my hands in the air. "It's not too much to ask." I sighed. "I gotta run, Tammie. The real estate agent is here, ready to hand me the keys."

"Okay, call me when you get settled."

"Will do."

I got out of my car and walked over to the overly chipper real estate agent, Sandra, standing by the door. "Hi," she practically sang. "You must be Sugar?"

"That I am."

"Awesome." She beamed. "I've got your keys for the bakery, and this extra set is for the studio apartment upstairs."

"Thanks so much," I said, trying to match her enthusiasm.

"Kinda cool, a girl named Sugar opening a bakery. Any idea what you'll call it?" she asked, flicking her long brown hair off her shoulder.

"Not yet," I replied and inwardly cringed at the endless questions.

"What do you specialize in?" she pressed, clearly not picking up on my lack of interest in small talk.

"Cookies," I said firmly. Though, in reality, I had no clue what I was doing.

If I asked Tammie, she'd tell me I specialized in nothing except crunching numbers at my boring corporate job in the city.

"Sugar's Cookies! That would be a cute name," she said, as if she'd just cracked the code to the universe.

I considered it for a moment. Maybe Sandra was onto something. "Yeah, that's kinda cute."

Sandra beamed, apparently pleased with herself. "Anyway, back to business. The Wi-Fi and tech guy will be coming later this week to set up your POS system and fix your Wi-Fi. His name's William, but everyone calls him Willie. He's a local, super nice, so if you need anything, just ask him."

If Willie the Wi-Fi Wizard was half as chatty as Sandra, I was in for a week of endless small talk.

We stepped inside the bakery, and I had to admit—it was amazing. Just needed a little sprucing up.

"Thank you," I mumbled, barely paying attention to Sandra now.

I was too busy being completely gobsmacked. The bakery was perfect . . . Well, mostly. It had all the charm of an old-school shop mixed with a hint of "needs some love." High ceilings, exposed brick walls, and big, sunny windows that practically begged to be admired. The counters had that "lived-in but still stylish" charm, and the faint scent of flour lingered in the air like a warm reminder of what this place used to be.

Sandra shot me a quick smile and a wave as she headed for the door. "I'll leave you to it," she called out, disappearing before I could muster a real response.

The sound of her heels clicking down the sidewalk was the only thing that snapped me out of my daze.

I wandered around the space, running my hand across the counters like I was already the head baker in some food network special. The ovens looked shiny and slightly intimidating, and the display cases sat empty, just waiting to be filled with whatever edible-ish masterpieces I could manage to not set on fire. This place had everything—well, everything except my personal touch and maybe a fire extinguisher.

I closed my eyes and took a deep breath. "Tomorrow, I'm going to learn how to bake."

No backing out now; it was do or dough.

Willie

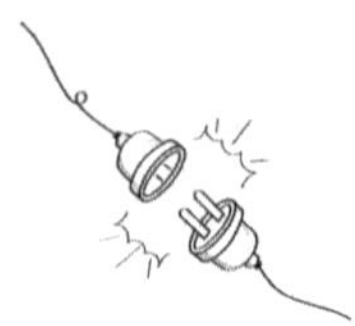

"Hi, Willie. Lovely Tuesday morning," Mrs. Newcastle chirped from her front door, waving like we were in a parade.

I gave her a quick nod and held up my work bag in a half-hearted wave, so she wouldn't think I was rude for not stopping to chat.

I'd lived in Rantucky my whole life—generations of my family had, actually. Small-town living had its perks and, well, its downsides. The upside? I knew for a fact that without even asking, Mrs. Newcastle would keep an eye on my house while I was off at work, and if I was running late, she'd probably pop over with leftovers from her dinner. That's just how people operated around here—everyone looked out for each other, whether you wanted them to or not.

The downside? Well, I was a forty-five-year-old tech guru, and most days I wished I had a wife to come home to, not a well-meaning little, old lady with a casserole dish. In a small town, once a rumor starts, it never really dies. It all kicked off because I decided to go to my first highschool party after graduation. I was freshly eighteen, eager to let loose before heading off to tech school. Back then, I was young, full of excitement, and a bit naive. That night, I lost my virginity, and what should've been an awkward, forgettable milestone ended up being the worst decision of my life.

The girl I was with decided to spread a rumor—a particularly cruel one that stuck in a town like Rantucky. She told everyone that my One-Eyed Trouser Trout was no bigger than her pinkie. I tried to laugh it off, deny it, set the record straight. Deep down, I knew there was a painful nugget of truth in what she said. Not pinkie-sized, no, but definitely more like an index finger.

But in a town like Rantucky, that tiny detail didn't matter. Once the rumor started, it spread faster than the town's gossip at bingo night, and before I knew it, I was the punchline of every joke.

"Wee Willie."

From then on, I was branded, and no girl wanted to be the one who dated the guy with the most unfortunate nickname in town.

Eventually, over the years and many failed attempts at dating, I decided I was destined to be alone. It was just me, and my hand, to keep me company.

I climbed into the truck and made my way toward Main Street. Setting up the bakery's Wi-Fi was familiar territory since I'd done it when they first opened ten years ago. But knowing the new owner was a city slicker had me feeling less than thrilled about the job.

I parked the truck, grabbed my toolbox, and hopped out. As soon as I saw the bright yellow sports car parked out front, I rolled my eyes. Every now and then, someone from the city would breeze in, thinking they could bring their big-city ways to Rantucky, but they never lasted. I wondered how long this one would hold out.

I glanced down at my clipboard and frowned. There wasn't a proper name listed for the owner—just one word: Sugar. That had to be some kind of mistake. Maybe the person who owned this place thought she was filling out her grocery list instead of the Wi-Fi install form.

I shook my head and then knocked on the door.

"Coming," a feminine voice shouted.

A second later, the door flew open, and there she was—like a hurricane wrapped in flour. Her wild brown hair looked like it had attempted to escape its ponytail and succeeded, with a generous sprinkling of flour tangled in the strands. Sweat glistened on her forehead, as if she'd just run a marathon, but it only made her glow in the soft light of the bakery.

Her big brown eyes were wide with a mix of panic and apology, but they sparkled with a kind of curiosity that drew me in. She had thick, plush lips, nestled like a bed I wanted to dive into. Honestly, I couldn't concentrate on anything other than her curves—plump and soft. This woman was a whirlwind of flour and chaos, and somehow the most beautiful person I'd ever laid eyes on.

"Uh, hi," she said, brushing some flour off her forehead. "You're here for the Wi-Fi, right? Sorry, I, uh . . . got a little too ambitious with the whole 'learning to bake' thing. Usually, I'm slightly less . . . dough covered."

I stood there, toolbox in hand, completely dumbstruck. "Learning to bake?" I asked, looking down at my clipboard to make sure I was at the right place.

How did a baker not know how to bake?

"Oh," she giggled, and it was the kind of sound that made my heart skip, like that moment when you finally get the modem to connect after fighting with it all day. "I bought this bakery on a whim, you know? Just chasing this big, sugar-coated dream. And now that I'm knee deep in flour and bills, I'm starting to wonder if I accidentally plugged the wrong cable into this whole 'life plan' thing."

There was no way she used an electric pun. *She might just be my dream girl.*

"Regret?" I asked, still standing awkwardly in the doorframe.

She shrugged. "Yeah, I just—" Suddenly, her face lit up, eyes wide with excitement as she bounced back into the bakery. "Oh, golly. Actually, come inside. You've got to try my new cream puff recipe and tell me what you think."

"Oh, uh, okay," I mumbled awkwardly. "And then I should get to work installing the Wifi."

She was already halfway to the kitchen, waving me off like the Wi-Fi was an afterthought. "Yeah, yeah, you're Willie, right?"

I winced a little, hoping she hadn't heard the story behind the nickname. People around here could be brutal. "Uh, yeah?"

She laughed again and glanced over her shoulder. "That sounded like you weren't sure if your name's Willie or not."

I chuckled, trying to shake off the awkwardness. "No, it's definitely Willie."

"Good. I'd hate for my first day in Rantucky to land me on some murder-mystery podcast," she said with a smirk. "Oh, by the way, my name's Sugar."

Wait—Sugar? So the name on the form wasn't a mistake after all.

I blinked. "Sugar? That's . . . kind of ironic," I said, glancing around the bakery.

She nodded casually and stopped right at the door that led to the kitchen. "Yeah, my parents died while baking sugar cookies. Super tragic."

The way she said it so nonchalantly, like she was talking about the weather instead of a family tragedy, left me momentarily speechless.

She just waved it off. "Yeah, it's whatever. People think I named myself after the incident, but no, they were just hippies who thought Sugar was a good idea for a baby name. So, you know, it's weird all around."

I didn't know whether to laugh or be concerned. "That's . . . a lot to unpack."

"Yeah, but hey, I'm opening a bakery now, so I guess I'm keeping the legacy alive. Just, uh, no sugar cookies on the menu." She grinned despite just dropping the most bizarre backstory I'd ever heard.

Sugar pushed through the wooden Dutch door and disappeared into the back. I took the opportunity to wander around, checking out the space. The wires I'd need for the Wi-Fi were still running along the ceiling like they had been for years. Aside from that, everything looked about the same—except it could definitely use a fresh coat of paint.

"Got 'em," she chirped as she reappeared, a tray in hand.

I eyed the tray and then the . . . blobs on it. "Cream puffs?" I asked, more out of hope than certainty, because what she was presenting looked more like a pastry crime scene than an actual dessert.

"Try one," she said, looking down at the tray and then back up to me.

She looked so excited, practically bouncing on her toes as she held out the tray, her eyes wide with anticipation. There was no way I could say no. So, against my better judgment, I grabbed one of the so-called "cream puffs" and brought it to my mouth, trying not to grimace at its doughy texture.

The moment it hit my tongue, I knew something was very, very wrong. Sour cream. It wasn't sweet at all—it was like I'd taken a bite out of a taco topping wrapped in half-baked dough. My brain screamed at me to spit it out, but her expectant gaze kept me from doing that. I swallowed, fighting back the gag, and forced a smile.

"Wow . . . this is . . . something," I managed, my voice strained from the effort of keeping it down.

Her face fell instantly, and her shoulders slumped as the excitement drained from her like air from a deflating balloon.

"It's terrible, isn't it?" she muttered, glaring at the tray like it had betrayed her.

I didn't have the heart to lie, but I also didn't want to crush her spirit. "Well, it's . . . unique. You're definitely on to something here . . . just not sure what that something is yet."

Tears welled up in her big brown eyes, and before I knew what I was doing, I dropped my toolbox and wrapped her in a tight hug. "Hey, now," I whispered softly, trying to comfort her as best I could. "It's not bad . . . it's maybe not your best? Everyone has off days."

But she shook her head, her tears spilling over. "No, you don't understand," she sobbed. "I'm not good at *anything*. I opened this bakery on a whim, thinking it would be this fresh start, and now . . . now, I have nothing to show for it. No one's going to buy anything from me. They'll all just think I'm some kind of fraud, pretending I know what I'm doing."

I stepped back, still holding her shoulders, and looked her in the eyes. "Whoa, whoa, hold up. You are *not* a fraud. You're new. No one's great at this stuff right away. Trust me. My first tech gig? I took down an entire office's internet by plugging the wrong dongle in the wrong port. And yeah, people thought I was an idiot for, like, a week. But then you learn and get better. It's just day one. Nobody nails cream puffs on day one."

I wasn't necessarily sure how she planned on getting a bakery up and running in a week, but maybe her other desserts were better.

She gave a little snort through her tears and wiped her nose with the back of her hand. "You really think I can do this?"

"Absolutely." I grinned. "I'd love to see what else you created."

She laughed, sniffling, and I swear it was the most beautiful, flour-covered giggle I'd ever heard. "The installation will take a few days, right?"

"Yes, but don't fret, you'll be all set for your opening next week." If she could figure out what to bake, that is.

"Perfect. Then I'll be able to bake you something new for tomorrow." She dusted off her hands against her apron. "Tell me more about what you need from me. You mentioned a dongle?"

Sugar

A blush crept over his cheeks, and he turned toward his little red metal toolbox. When he turned around with some wires and a few tools I didn't recognize in his hand, it was the first time I got to really take in his appearance. Willie was tall and lanky, with a big beard that framed his face. His metal-framed glasses, the kind that seemed almost too big for his face, added to his quirky charm. Despite his height, there was something almost gentle about him, especially when he blushed. It was like watching a big, awkward bear trying to hide behind those glasses and all that facial hair.

He was really cute and definitely someone I would go after back in Chicago, if I hadn't sworn off dating.

"Yeah, do you mind if we go upstairs to the electrical box? It's in the studio upstairs."

"Sure," I said, shrugging.

He'd already proven he wasn't going to murder me and was here to do his job, so might as well.

I knew those cream puffs were going to be another disaster to add to my growing list of baking fails, but Willie was so sweet about letting me down gently—much kinder than Tammie would've been.

"Alright then," he mused, and we headed up to the studio apartment.

Fortunately, the owners before me left it furnished, and I'd stuffed my suitcases into the bedroom.

"I, uh, just need to use the electrical panel here." He pointed to a gray box on the wall in the entryway when I opened the door.

"Sounds good," I commented. "Mind if I watch?"

"You want to watch?" he asked.

I shrugged. "I don't know anything about tech stuff, and I can't be calling you every single day, so I might as well learn."

That was the motto of my new life: no more depending on people to fix my problems. I was going to be my own fixer-upper, solving things one disaster at a time. This was the new me—living solo and chasing a dream my parents would be proud of.

"I could swing by and help," Willie offered as he popped open the panel, revealing a tangled mess of wires.

"Wow," I said, staring at the chaos. "That's . . . a lot of configuring."

He let out a laugh, low and rough, and I found myself giving him another once-over. Had he somehow gotten more attractive after opening up the electrical panel? Ugh. Why did I have to develop a crush right after declaring my vow of celibacy?

I wasn't going to get involved with any man—not after a lifetime of disappointment. And judging by how tall Willie was, I bet he'd just add another complication with his, well . . . *overcompensating anatomy.* The last thing I needed was another "too big" problem.

Willie crouched in front of the panel and carefully sorted through the jumble of wires. "See here?" he said, his voice low and steady. "These two wires"—he pointed to a red one and a blue one twisted together in some kind of electrical tango—"they're not supposed to be crossed like this. I just need to separate them, then connect them to the right terminals, and then I'll be able to start the install downstairs."

He glanced back at me over his shoulder, those big metal glasses sliding down his nose a little. The way he explained it, so calm, so sure of himself, had my brain short-circuiting in a way that had nothing to do with the panel in front of us.

Willie moved his fingers—his index and middle—with slow, deliberate grace as he separated the wires, almost like he was caressing them. The way he slid his fingers over the wires, guiding them apart with such care, made the whole thing feel unexpectedly sensual.

Why was this so sexy? Was I broken? Was I actually turned on by someone explaining the inner workings of Wi-Fi? Apparently, yes. Yes, I was. Maybe it was the way he looked at the panel like he was about to conquer it—or maybe it was the way he effortlessly moved his hands through the chaos.

I needed to get laid. I'd have to put on my favorite video and use the rainbow vibrator later because there was no way I was actually getting all randy about a man touching wires.

"I'll just connect these two," he said, his voice still low, "and we'll head downstairs to test it out."

"Is this the dongle you were talking about?" I peered over his shoulder and into the box that he was configuring.

"The, uh . . .what?" he asked, flustered.

I quickly pulled away when I realized how close I was to him.

"The dongle," I giggled. "You said in your first tech job you got the dongles confused so—"

"Please, stop using the word . . . dongle." His eyes were focused on the wires, but a distinct redness was spreading across the back of his neck.

He was getting flustered. Absolutely and utterly flustered. I sat in silence for a few more minutes as he worked his fingers around the wires. He was so meticulous. He used his forefinger and middle finger to glide over the wires, stroking them with precision.

"Tell me about the bakery," he asked, but his voice held a thick rasp that wasn't there earlier.

Did he feel what I felt too?

"I started it because I really want people to have a place to come and feel a sense of community." I hesitated. "But the truth is I want to live up to my name. I want to be the Sugar my parents would be proud of."

"I bet they'd be really proud if they could see what you're doing now." He glanced over his shoulder, and the redness had subsided . . . slightly.

"Thanks," I said softly and then turned back to what his fingers were doing.

This conversation was getting too heavy. Willie seemed to notice the shift in the tension and went back to finish what he was doing about the wires.

"So if I connect the red wire to the yellow and gently wrap them around each other . . ."

Willie's voice was low and focused, but all I could concentrate on were his fingers. His thumb joined the show, and suddenly, his hands on those wires felt way more intimate than they had any right to. He moved his fingers in a slow, almost teasing way, guiding the wires together with a light touch that had my mind wandering into dangerous territory.

I imagined those fingers on me instead of the wires, tracing that same deliberate path down my body. The way he pressed with his thumb, coaxing the connection, had me wondering how it would feel to have him guiding *me* to that kind of spark. Why did I suddenly feel like I was the one he was trying to turn on, not the Wi-Fi?

"You're so good at that," I praised.

A low rumble echoed from his chest.

"Tell me what you've tried baking." That gruff voice was back.

"Well, I've tried making brownies, pies . . ." My breasts pressed against his back as I tried to get a closer view. "I tried to make this cream pie—"

In an instant, Willie turned around, and before I could blink or even remember how breathing worked, his lips were on mine. One second, I was talking about cream pies and the next, I was in a full-on kiss with the lanky, bearded tech guy who'd suddenly gone rogue.

His lips were firm and determined, like he was trying to fix a connection problem that had nothing to do with Wi-Fi. My brain went into overdrive, half panicking, half thinking.

Is this really happening?

It was a kiss that took me by surprise, but I wasn't complaining.

He sat down and pulled me onto his lap, groaning into my mouth. "Talk about cream pies again, tell me about them."

He brought his fingers to my chin, and I was confused about what he was asking.

"Tell me about the cream, Sugar," he demanded, mouth pressed against my neck.

"Oh," I blurted out awkwardly, realizing he wasn't talking about the actual pies I'd baked. He was definitely in a . . . different mood. "Well," I started to say, but instead of continuing, my body instinctively moved against him, grinding against his jeans.

I was searching for that telltale bulge, but it wasn't as obvious as I'd imagined it would be. I made a mental note of that.

"I made the crust," I whispered, my hips moving in sync with the growing tension. "The key is getting it just right—golden on the outside, soft and warm in the middle . . . ready to hold whatever's coming next."

He groaned low in his throat, tightening his fingers at my waist as he licked up my neck. "And the filling?" His voice was rough, thick with want.

I leaned in closer, my breath hot against his ear. "Thick . . . rich . . . creamy. You've got to take your time, make sure it's smooth, stirring it just right until it's ready to be poured in."

His hips pressed back against mine as I ground against him. "I think I'm ready for a taste," he rasped.

I smirked, my body moving against him with purpose now. "Looks like we're both working on filling that pie," I murmured, my voice laced with a mix of teasing and desire.

Sliding my hands down his chest, I could feel him responding, ready to cream this pie just as much as I was ready to take it.

"You'd like that, wouldn't you?" he murmured. "You want me to take a little taste of your cookie, Sugar?"

"Mm-hmm," I purred. "Go ahead, taste how sweet it can be."

His voice dropped even lower, teasing. "All slick and wet, just waiting for a little flour to mix in?"

My nipples hardened beneath his touch, and I couldn't help but smirk. "Add your banana to the batter, Willie, and we might just whip up my signature recipe."

He groaned softly against my neck, his lips brushing my skin as he nibbled, sending shivers down my spine.

"Take off your pants, Sugar," he growled, the playful edge still there. "Let me get a taste of that sweetness."

I stood up slowly, and he followed, matching my movements. His eyes were locked on mine like we were about to bake something a whole lot hotter than pies.

I led him through the small studio toward the bed tucked in the corner of the room. I turned to face him and held his gaze as I slowly slid my pants down, feeling them glide over my skin and drop to the floor.

I'd sworn off big dicks, but a guy with a tongue like Willie's? Sometimes, a girl just has to make an exception for the right kind of tool.

Glasses fogging up from the heat between us, he took a shaky breath and pressed them up his nose, never breaking eye contact. His eyes were hungry, devouring every inch of me as I stood exposed in front of him.

"Lie down," he said, voice low and rough. "Spread-eagle."

I climbed onto the bed and settled into the position with a little more sass than was probably necessary, legs spread wide, my heart racing. Willie dropped to his knees, eyes locked on me, his face just inches from my Beaver. The intensity of his stare had me nearly squirming, but I held still, feeling his breath on my skin.

"Let me inspect your electrical box, Sugar," he murmured, sliding his hands up my thighs, his touch light and teasing. "See if we've got some wires that need uncrossing."

His fingers hovered, close enough to drive me wild, and the way he said it—like he was about to work some serious magic—made my whole body hum with anticipation. Who knew getting an "inspection" could be this exciting?

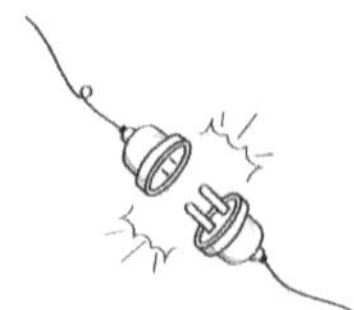

Willie

My body thrummed with energy as I knelt in front of her and stared down at the hot, wet pussy practically dripping with anticipation. It had been a long time since I'd been this close to a woman, and the sheer intensity of it had me on edge, like a live wire about to spark.

I wanted to devour her, but at the same time, I knew I needed to savor every inch, every taste.

Her voice broke through my haze, playful and dripping with desire. "Give me that Tonsil Inspector, Willie. Lick me clean like you just finished a good cream pie."

I swallowed hard and pushed my glasses up as high as they'd go. With her permission hanging in the air like a challenge, I dove in headfirst, exploring her with my tongue like she was the sweetest dessert I'd ever had the pleasure of tasting.

"Let me see where those wires are crossed, Sugar."

My tongue slid against her, and the taste was intoxicating—warm, sweet, and salty all at once. It was like the perfect mix of flavors I didn't even know I craved until now. I pressed my tongue flat, licking a slow, deliberate line up her wetness, savoring every inch. Her slick heat was enough to make my head spin, my glasses fogging up all over again, but I didn't care.

"Yes, Willie. Use those fingers and uncross them for me."

I circled my tongue around her clit, and her body twitched in response. A low groan escaped me. The sound of my tongue sliding against her, the wet slurps as I licked and teased, filled the room with an obscene, messy rhythm. I couldn't get enough, and every time I sucked her clit into my mouth, she gasped, making me want more.

I added a finger into her wet heat. "You're so sweet, Sugar."

Like I was finger fucking a wet strawberry pie, I circled her pussy and watched her writhe beneath my hand.

My tongue was on overdrive, slurping and lapping. I was practically drowning in her wetness, but I craved more with every second. It was messy, obscene, and perfect. Each lick, each suck, pulled out more of that sweetness, and I was a man on a mission to drink her sweetness dry.

Her moans were wild, mixing with the ridiculous slurping sounds I was making—heck, I sounded like I was trying to finish the last bit of milkshake through a straw, but I didn't care. The messier, the better. I flicked my tongue faster, swirling around her clit like I was trying to win the State Fair pussy-eating contest. Her taste was addictive.

"You're so good with your mouth, Willie."

I plunged back inside her, fucking her sweet hole with my hands like it was the last thing I was ever going to touch. She might be the only person who didn't know my nickname in this town, and I sure wasn't going to be the one to tell her.

"God, Willie," she mewled.

Her hair was splayed out around her as she arched her hips, thrusting against my mouth and fingers.

"Slurp me like I'm a glass of milk with dessert," she commanded, and I didn't need to be told twice.

I took her clit into my mouth and sucked with all the force I could muster, making her squirm and scream out in pleasure.

"Yes," she screamed, and then it hit me—literally.

A rush of warm liquid sprayed all over my face, catching me off guard. It soaked my face and got all over my glasses, drenching everything. I didn't stop, though—I doubled down. Licking and sucking, I rode the wave of her release as it just kept going, turning me into a very, very happy mess.

She collapsed onto the bed, breathless, as I pulled away and wiped the liquid off my face. I strode toward the sink in the corner of the apartment and flicked on the water. Just as I started rinsing my glasses, she sprang up from the bed.

"Oh my goodness gracious, I'm so embarrassed," she blurted out.

I washed my face, grabbed a towel, and soaked it with water before turning back to her.

"Why?" I asked, genuinely confused.

"I-I've never done that before," Sugar mumbled, her cheeks turning pink as she sat back down. She was flustered and adorably sheepish.

I caught sight of her still-throbbing, red-hot pussy, and—*boom* —I was hard all over again. I was definitely going to need some serious alone time after this.

"Done what?" I asked, trying to play it cool.

"Squirted on anyone before," she confessed. "It was like a geyser went off, and I couldn't stop it."

I chuckled, walking over to her with the wet towel in hand. "I liked it," I said with a grin as I gently wiped her down, cleaning up the remnants of our little adventure. "And . . . I like you, Sugar."

Her face lit up with the biggest, most joyful smile I'd ever seen.

The whole room glowed with her happiness. It was impossible not to smile back. It felt like this was the best mess I'd ever gotten myself into.

"I like you too, Willie."

I cleaned her up quietly and stood when I was done, but she grabbed my hand and dropped to her knees in front of me.

"What're you doing?" I asked, looking down at her.

As much as I loved the sight of her kneeling before me, looking up at me with those big, eager eyes, I couldn't let her get that close—couldn't let her open my pants. The moment she did, she'd be gone, running for the hills.

"I want to help you out," she said with a sweet smile. "After that . . . well, one of the best orgasms of my life, I owe you."

Panic gripped me, and I shook my head quickly. "No," I blurted, trying to keep my cool. "I-I'm okay, really."

I glanced toward the door, searching for an escape route. "Thanks, but I . . . uh . . . I've got to finish up and head to another job today."

Total lie. I never double-booked anything, but right now, I didn't know what else to say. There was no way I could let her get any closer. As much as I wanted her mouth on me, I couldn't let her touch me. Couldn't let her undo my pants because then she'd know. She'd see the truth. She'd see my *Wee Willie* and realize what a fraud I was.

I could already picture the look on her face—either the pity or the laughter, neither of which I could handle. I'd been down that road before, and I wasn't about to subject myself to that again. I couldn't let her see my index finger–sized package and laugh.

"I'm sorry," I muttered. "I shouldn't have crossed that line with you."

Sugar looked up at me. "I wanted it. I promise. I want to please you."

I dropped my eyes to the floor. "I really have to go," I said, backing away.

Without another word, I turned and headed for the door, practically running downstairs. The Wi-Fi could wait until tomorrow. Right now, I needed to get home and try to stop thinking about all the ways I wanted Sugar all over me—ways I couldn't let happen.

Sugar

That orgasm must've unlocked some hidden creative side of me because I spent the entire evening—and well into the early morning—baking batch after batch of chocolate chip cookies. By the time the sun came up, I'd finally nailed a recipe I thought was *the one*. I called Tammie to share the news, but, as expected, she was skeptical. She told me I needed a second opinion before I opened a bakery that only sold chocolate chip cookies.

I pulled my hair into a ponytail and swiped on some mascara, glancing at the clock every few minutes, waiting for it to hit eight a.m.

As I watched the clock, I kept replaying the moment in my head, trying to figure out what had made him pull back so fast yesterday. I was ready to return the favor, to show him just how grateful I was for that mind-blowing orgasm, but he didn't even give me the chance. And the thing was, I was *really* willing to look past whatever was going on with his big wanker situation. Yeah, I've had my share of issues with oversized anatomy, but I was more curious about Willie than anything else. Something about him just made me want to stick around, made me want to . . . figure him out.

This morning, my attention was on the cookies. I'd been up all night perfecting the recipe, and I couldn't wait for him to try them. The idea of him tasting my cookies made me more excited than I cared to admit. The cookies had to be perfect, and I couldn't wait to see how he'd react. Would he show up? Would he actually want to try them? My heart raced a little at the thought, and not just because of the cookies.

Sure enough, at eight on the dot, the door creaked open, and there he was—Willie, standing in the doorway. He was in a black shirt that clung to his frame, just enough to show off those lean muscles, and a pair of gray sweat joggers that, well, let's just say they caught my attention instantly. His familiar red toolbox was in hand, and for a second, I wondered if that thing ever left his side.

My mouth dropped open, and I didn't even try to hide my surprise at how ridiculously good he looked. I mean, *joggers*. I've heard stories about what gray sweatpants are supposed to reveal, so naturally, my eyes went straight to his junk, my brain laser focused on seeing some kind of outline, *any* outline. But there was nothing. Absolutely nothing. I stared harder, squinting like I was trying to solve a mystery, but nope—nada, zip.

Where was his schlong? Was there really nothing there, or had he figured out some kind of sorcery to hide it all? Either way, I was in full-on investigation mode when his voice snapped me out of it.

"Hey, Sugar," he said.

That low, gruff voice from yesterday wrapped around me like a warm blanket, melting away any semblance of cool I had left. It was like he had no idea the effect he had on me—completely unaware that his voice alone could make my panties slide right off.

I blinked a few times, trying to shake off the daze. "Hey, Willie." I cleared my throat and attempted to sound casual. "Right on time." I tried not to let my voice betray the fact that I was just ogling him.

He smiled and set his toolbox down on the counter. "Yeah, figured I'd better stick to my word." His eyes flickered around the room before landing back on me. "Something smells good in here."

I grinned, finally getting my brain back on track. "Chocolate chip cookies. Freshly baked," I said, gesturing to the tray on the counter. "I might've perfected the recipe."

He raised an eyebrow, clearly intrigued and maybe slightly hesitant. "Now that's something I have to try."

I smiled. "Try one."

Willie reached out, wrapping his large fingers around one of the cookies. My eyes followed the movement as he slowly lifted the cookie to his mouth. The way his fingers gently broke off a piece, his thumb brushing against the soft, warm dough, sent a shiver through me.

He took a bite, and I was mesmerized as his lips closed around the cookie, his jaw moving with deliberate slowness. The sound of him biting into it was soft, but the way he chewed—his eyes fluttering closed for a brief moment—made the air around us feel heavy. His tongue darted out to catch a crumb on the corner of his mouth, and my pulse quickened.

"Mmm," he groaned low in his throat, the sound vibrating through me. He opened his eyes, locking them on mine as he took another slow bite. His lips wrapped around the cookie again, his jaw clenching as he chewed. "This is better than yesterday."

I threw the dish of cookies in the corner, not caring about flying glass, and rushed toward him. Willie's eyes went wide for a moment, but as I pressed my lips against his, he wrapped his arms around me.

"I kept thinking about you all night."

"Oh yeah?" he asked gruffly.

"Yeah," I murmured into his mouth.

"What were you thinking?"

"I was thinking about how good it'd feel if your dongle went into my floppy disk." I whimpered as I nibbled on his lower lip.

He pulled away from me, physically taking a large step backward, and coughed a few times.

"Oh." My cheeks reddened. "Did I say something wrong?"

"No." His voice gave him away. He still had that rough, raspy tone, the same one he had when he was busy eating my kitty.

"What's wrong?" I asked genuinely.

He shook his head, glancing nervously toward the large floor-to-ceiling windows at the front of the shop. "We're just downstairs. Anyone could see," he muttered, turning back to me with a worried expression.

I tilted my head, trying to ease the tension in the room. "We can go up to my apartment," I offered, attempting to solve the problem. "I could use some help getting those wires untangled again," I added with a playful smile, hoping to lighten the mood.

But his mouth stayed downturned, his expression still serious.

"I-I have a confession to make," he stammered.

His words were so serious that my heart gave a small, concerned flutter.

"Let's go upstairs," I suggested softly. "I'll put on some coffee to go with our cookies, and we can talk privately up there. How does that sound?"

He gave a small nod and followed me silently through the cafe and to the kitchen, where I grabbed more of the cookies before making my way up the narrow staircase to my small apartment. I pushed the door open as I led him inside and didn't bother locking it. The familiar space felt even smaller with the tension hanging in the air. I moved toward the kitchen, busied myself with the coffee, and tried to act casual.

He sat on the green worn-in sofa on the other side of my bed. I put some of the cookies on a plate and brought it over with the coffee.

"What's going on, Willie?" I asked and gestured to the dessert on the table.

He took a few long pulls of the warm liquid before putting it down. "I can't have sex with you."

My heart sank. I was hoping he wouldn't say that, but at the same time, I expected him to.

"Oh," I sighed and turned around.

This was for the best. It had to be because I'd have to use my vibrator afterward. I swore off big dicks anyway.

He grabbed my arms and spun me so I was facing him. "It's not . . . that." He closed his eyes and then opened them and grabbed my waist. "I, uh, I'm . . .."

He looked down at his body. I followed his line of sight and stared at his gray sweats. There was absolutely no outline where his Giggle Pin should be, and I was half tempted to lean down to get a closer look when he cleared his throat, and I brought my eyesight back up.

"I can't have sex with you because I'm not . . . well endowed."

Willie

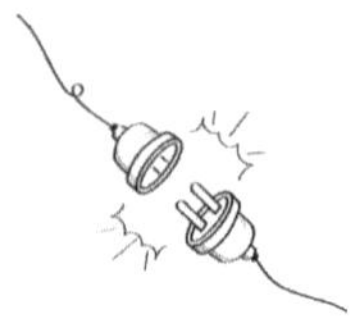

There it was. I'd said it. My face burned bright red from the neck up, and I instinctively reached for my toolbox, ready to bolt, when Sugar's delicate fingers wrapped around my elbow, stopping me in my tracks.

"What did you say?" she asked, her voice soft but curious.

Please don't make me say it again. It was humiliating enough the first time, and I didn't think I could handle repeating it.

But, fudge it. I let the words tumble out. "I have a little Rooster," I blurted, feeling the heat rise even higher in my cheeks. "When I lost my virginity, the girl started this rumor that I had a Wee Willie and claimed my . . . Fiddlestick was the size of a pinkie finger." I winced. "Which is a complete lie, by the way. It's more like an index finger. But either way, no one around here would ever touch me again. Who wants to sleep with the guy known for having a small dick?"

I couldn't stop. It was like my brain had cut the brakes. "It's not like . . . *tiny* tiny. I mean, yeah, when it's flaccid, it's not impressive. But I'm a grower, not a shower. I know what I'm doing—I promise. No one's ever stuck around long enough to figure that out, though."

I stared at the floor, waiting for the ground to swallow me whole while also wondering if I'd just made the worst sales pitch of my life.

The silence that followed was suffocating. It hung between us like a thick, awkward fog, wrapping itself around every word I had just vomited out. I stood frozen, desperate to say *something*, anything that would let me escape the mess I'd just made. My face was burning, and all I could think about was leaving, getting out of here before this became any worse. I needed to tell her to find someone else to install her Wi-Fi and POS system—someone better, someone who didn't come with baggage and a "Wee Willie" reputation.

Just as I was turning to make my exit, she grabbed onto my waistband. Before I could even process what was happening, her lips—thick, plush lips—kissed me.

I froze, my brain short-circuiting. Complete shock. My eyes went wide, and for a split second, I was certain I was imagining things. She pressed her mouth against me, taking me in deeper, her lips gliding over me with such ease, like she couldn't wait to prove every word I'd said wrong.

"Thank God," she murmured against me, her lips vibrating as she spoke.

The sensation was overwhelming, sending a shockwave through my entire body.

I blinked as my mind struggled to catch up.

Was this real? Was this actually happening?

I pulled away. "I-I am so confused. I'm not sure if you heard me right, but—"

She pressed a finger to my lips, silencing me. "No. I heard you. Thank fuck I heard you."

I shook my head, utterly baffled. "I'm so confused."

"Explain later," she said, grabbing a cookie with a cheeky grin. "Eat my cookie, Willie."

Where has this woman been all my life? I just confessed to having a small Baguette, and she *still* wanted to see it? It was like I'd stumbled into some alternate universe where none of my worst fears applied.

"Happily," I replied.

My heart was pounding, but somehow I felt . . . excited. Maybe this was actually happening.

"I need you to put your frosting on my cookie, Willie," she teased.

I couldn't help but grin as the heat between us built. "You need me to check if that floppy disk still works?" I asked, my voice dropping to a husky murmur. "Because I've been thinking . . . I might've forgotten to add more power to the circuit."

Her eyes sparkled with amusement. "Yes, but only if I get a taste of that Sour Cream Rifle."

I hesitated for just a moment.

Was I really ready for this?

I'd laid it all out there, no filter, no excuses, and she still hadn't run. But once she saw it, would she change her mind? Maybe if I made sure she was completely satisfied first, she'd look past my . . . less-than-ideal situation.

I took a deep breath, determined. If she wasn't running now, I wasn't about to give her a reason to.

"Can you take off your clothes?" I asked. She nodded repeatedly and pulled off everything. She stood in front of me, bare in all her glory.

I lifted her around the waist and tossed her onto the table, noticing place settings were neatly set up at each chair. "Were you expecting someone?"

She shook her head, blushing. "N-no. I just like to have it set up. It makes me feel like my day's in order when everything's organized."

Without another word, I walked to the kitchen, leaving her perched curiously on the table. I grabbed a pair of metal tongs and a spatula, then placed them next to her on the table, watching her reaction.

"Willie," she moaned. "Yes. I want to be served to you. If you're lucky, you can have dessert first."

I shifted her and lifted her hips just enough to slide the plate under her butt, making sure it was positioned just right. "Perfect," I muttered, as if I were plating a five-star meal.

Her breath hitched, eyes locked on me, and I grabbed the metal tongs, clicking them together playfully before using them to gently spread her pussy lips.

I set the tongs down beside her, then picked up the fork and spoon at my place setting, giving them a little spin in my fingers like I was about to dive into a gourmet feast. Pulling up a chair, I took my seat and tapped the fork against the spoon, unable to hide the grin spreading across my face.

"Alright," I said, leaning in closer, "I'm ready to eat my meal. Table's set, and I'm starving."

"You do realize you're not eating dinner, right? This is dessert."

I shot her a cheeky grin. "If you're my dessert, then I'm going to eat it at the table like the good boy I am."

She moaned, and the sound drove me wild. "You *are* my good boy. Now eat that sweet treat."

Without hesitation, I spread her legs wide and lowered myself between them. My face hovered inches from her glistening pussy, the heat radiating off her making my mouth water.

"I'm going to make sure I get every single bite," I whispered, pushing my glasses up before diving in.

My tongue immediately found her clit, lapping and sucking in exactly the way I knew she liked from yesterday. Her taste was intoxicating, and I couldn't get enough. Each time I sucked harder, she moaned louder, her hips bucking against my mouth as I buried myself deeper, determined to eat my snack.

She bucked harder, and I tightened my grip on her thighs, holding her steady as I flicked my tongue faster. Her wetness coated my lips, and I couldn't help but groan against her, the sound vibrating through her as she cried out, pushing herself closer to the edge.

I alternated between sucking and licking, determined to bring her over that cliff. Her body trembled, thighs quivering around my head, and then she let out a sharp gasp as her orgasm ripped through her. Her legs tightened around me, but I didn't stop. I lapped up every bit of her release, working her through the waves of pleasure with my tongue.

As I pulled away, wiping my mouth with the back of my hand, I couldn't help but shoot her a grin. "Told you I'd get every morsel. You don't leave a crumb behind when dessert's that good."

She laughed, still breathless, her chest rising and falling. "Well, you definitely earned your treat."

I leaned back in the chair, raising an eyebrow. "I'm starting to think I should open a bakery of my own. Call it Willie's Sweet Treats. First item on the menu: *You*."

She snorted. "Oh, please."

I smirked and stood up, leaning closer to her and sliding my hands up her thighs. "I'm pretty good at . . . taste testing."

Her eyes twinkled. "Well, I hope your taste-testing skills extend to more than just cookies, Willie."

"Oh, I assure you, I'm a man of many talents," I teased, kissing the inside of her thigh. "And I haven't even gotten started on the frosting yet."

She ran her fingers through my hair, grinning. "Alright, *good boy*. But if you're gonna be that good, maybe we should work on our next recipe . . . away from the dining table."

"Are you sure?" I asked.

She just nodded and slid off the table. I loved the way she dripped down her thigh.

"Please let me." Her eyes sparkled. "Let me see your Weiner, Willie."

Sugar

When he told me he had a tiny Johnson, I thought for sure he was trolling me. I mean, *really*? A guy this tall with a small member? No way. But the more embarrassed he got about it, the more I realized that maybe I had stumbled upon the gold at the end of the rainbow. After swearing off men for so long, here I was, in Rantucky of all places, opening a bakery on a whim and possibly finding exactly what I didn't even know I wanted.

"Let me see it," I demanded, my voice breathless with anticipation.

My mouth was watering for him. I was ready, so ready for his Sausage.

I grabbed his hands and shoved him back against the door. If I made the perfect chocolate chip cookie batch after yesterday, I couldn't imagine what I'd conjure after this. I was aching for him.

"I've waited so long to find someone like you, Willie."

I grabbed the waistband of his gray joggers and pulled them down. He stepped out of them, and then, like a cat, I prowled toward him and grabbed the hem of his boxers.

He took my hands, stopping me momentarily. "I can't have this be a letdown, Sugar."

I shook my head. "No." I reached up and trailed my nails gently along his body, watching his breath hitch. "You don't understand. Everybody deserves to be loved and celebrated. You should never feel embarrassed. I want to make you feel good, Willie, because you make me feel so good."

A slow smile crept across his face, softening the tension. "Okay, Sugar," he said, finally letting go of my hands, the hesitation starting to melt away.

"But only if you make me a promise," I teased, biting my lip as I leaned in closer.

"What's that?"

"You have to promise to give me a good cream pie for dessert after this." I winked.

His grin widened as he raised an eyebrow. "You want me to douse you *à la mode*?" Willie crooned.

"Please." I whimpered, the anticipation almost too much as I hooked my fingers into his waistband and pulled his boxers off.

As his boxers dropped, a surge of excitement rushed through me. There it was—his Pearl Jammer—and he hadn't been kidding. It was small and rested against him, flaccid despite the fact that I could feel his desire radiating off him. Pure, unfiltered arousal filled me. The vulnerability, the softness—it made me want him even more. He was everything I watched in the films I loved, and I was surprised that I was living out my fantasy.

I smiled up at him. He started to say something, clearly flustered, but I didn't want to hear it.

I grabbed the spatula, slipped it underneath his tiny length, and gave it a wiggle. The way it rested there, wobbling like a Jell-O dessert waiting to be devoured, made me grin wider.

"Oh, look at this," I teased, tilting my head as if inspecting a fancy pastry. "You're just begging to be frosted."

Without breaking eye contact, I dropped to my knees and leaned in. I dragged my tongue along his length, feeling him twitch with every movement. The spatula held him perfectly in place.

I paused, licking my lips and savoring the taste. "Mmm," I hummed, "this might be my new favorite recipe."

I gave him one last slow lick, gliding my tongue from base to tip, before letting him drop back down with a soft *plop*. I threw the spatula down. "But seriously," I said, raising an eyebrow, "if you don't behave, I'm going to start calling you Shortbread."

His groan was delicious. "Sugar—"

"Shh," I whispered, grinning. "Let me get this Pipe Cleaner in my mouth and show you just how happy I am right now."

Without hesitation, I took him into my mouth, loving how soft and smooth he felt against my lips. There was something so perfect about it, about being able to take all of him, savoring every inch as I wrapped my tongue fully around him. His skin was warm, and the softness was a turn-on in a way I hadn't anticipated. The way his body responded to me was exhilarating. I was going to make him feel as good as he made me feel.

I swirled my tongue around his smooth skin and slid my hand down. Gently cupping his wrinkled berries, I applied a little pressure, relishing their soft weight. He moaned, and the sound vibrated through me, giving me all the permission I needed. I gripped his Joystick with my mouth and gave it a firm, teasing tug, coaxing him further.

With each movement, I could feel the subtle shift in him. His shaft, still soft, started to respond, a slow build of pressure growing beneath my tongue. I took him deeper, eager to feel him fully come to life in my mouth, and I loved every second of this sweet, slow transformation. His moans grew louder, and he shifted his hips forward as he shoved himself farther into my mouth.

The bigger he grew, the more I realized he was right. He was about the length of my index finger, and it was everything and more.

I pulled away from him, holding it in my hand and loving the way it fit in my palm. I coaxed and caressed his Top Hat as he groaned above me.

"I'm going to stick your dongle into my cum dumpster now."

"Fuck, Sugar. Your mouth is as sweet as your cunt."

I leaned forward and circled my tongue around his head. He didn't hit the back of my throat like the other men did. I didn't have to extend my jaw or hurt myself. It was the . . .

"Perfect lollipop," I crooned as I tugged harder on him.

He was fully erect now. I popped on and off, alternating between rubbing down his frenulum and sticking him in my mouth. I sucked on him so hard that I thought I was going to suck the jizz right out of him.

He gently gathered my sweaty hair, pulling it back from my face. "What a good handlebar you make," Willie groaned.

I kept working him with my mouth, using my hands to maintain a steady rhythm. His length made it easy for me to pull away, but my fingers ensured the friction he needed to finish.

"Fudgesicle," he moaned and gripped my ponytail tightly. "I'm going to—"

Hot, wet ropes of cum spilled onto my tongue, and I eagerly lapped it up like the sweetest treat. He released his grip on my hair as I smeared his release across my face, almost like soothing Chap-Stick on parched lips..

"Tastes like sticky toffee pudding," I purred, earning a grin from him.

He dropped to his knees in front of me, bringing us face to face, before pressing his lips to mine in a deep, tender kiss.

"Are you okay?" he asked softly, his gaze searching mine.

I nodded, feeling far more than okay. This was hands down the best oral I'd ever experienced—giving or receiving. I'd do it for him again in a heartbeat. "More than okay."

He lifted me with a grin and carried me toward my tiny bathroom. "Let's get you cleaned up before you set like overbaked brownies."

We squeezed into the small space, bumping into the counter. "Welcome to my high-tech lair," I said, flicking the light on. "Where the wires are old and the outlets are questionable."

"Yeah, it feels like a place where I'd get electrocuted for plugging in a toaster," he teased, eyeing the buzzing light above us.

We took turns rinsing each other off, giggling as the showerhead sputtered to life like it was short-circuiting.

"Might want to check the wiring in here," he joked, ducking as water sprayed randomly.

We scrubbed away the evidence of our fun, washing and laughing, while the bathroom steamed up.

After we finished, I pulled on a summer dress with a new pair of underwear. Willie was sitting at the table with his clothes on. His hair was slicked back, and he still had a little sheen on his glasses.

"So, are you gonna tell me I need to leave?" he asked, though his tone was more playful than usual.

I shook my head and pulled up a chair beside him. I was ready to share my story. After all this time of keeping things to myself, I trusted him enough to open up. It wasn't easy, but I knew I needed to say it out loud. "I swore off men when I moved out here."

"Why?"

I ran my hands through my hair. "The big-city guys with their big egos and their big Semen Spitters—I couldn't stand them," I said. "Too large, too much. I mean, they act like they're doing you a favor, and their egos? Even worse. I needed to get away, so I left the city to escape it all."

He paused, eyebrows raised, then looked at me. "So . . . my anatomy is attractive to you?"

"Makes me wet," I deadpanned. With a smirk, I added, "I'm still waiting for you to give my Squish Mitten your pie filling."

"Happily. I will—"

Suddenly, it hit me like a bolt of lightning. "Oh my, the recipe." I leaped out of the chair, practically vibrating with excitement. "Sorry!" I screeched, already halfway to the door. "I've gotta bake."

I grabbed the pad and pen I kept stashed by the door for moments just like this. "You can handle that electrical stuff, right?" I called over my shoulder, barely waiting for a response.

"Uh-huh," Willie chuckled, amused, as I dashed out of the apartment and straight to the bakery kitchen, my brain buzzing with sweet inspiration.

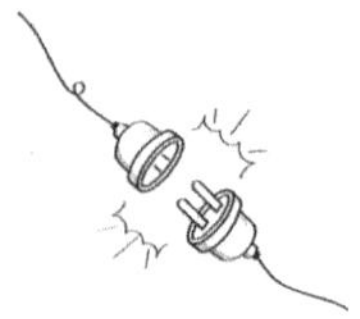

Willie

The job took longer than I expected today, probably because we were a little distracted this morning. I hadn't seen much of Sugar since she dashed out of her apartment earlier. By the time I wrapped things up, it was well past five. The only thing left to install was the POS system.

I headed out to my truck to put my tools away and grabbed the couple of gallons of paint I'd picked up from the hardware store last night.

"Sugar?" I called, leaning into the kitchen to see if she was around.

The kitchen was a complete disaster zone. Flour dusted every surface, mixing bowls and utensils were scattered haphazardly across the countertops, and crumpled recipe notes were strewn everywhere. The chaos reminded me of an electrical panel mid-repair—wires hanging out, tools spread in every direction, and no clear path to what was working and what wasn't. There were half-finished pastries and trays stacked on top of each other.

Sugar was hunched over the oven, completely absorbed in whatever creation she was baking. Her hair was pulled up in a messy bun, strands sticking out in all directions, and her focus was so intense that I didn't want to disturb her.

I slipped out quietly and decided to start painting the bakery. I already knew what color she'd picked—a soft lilac—thanks to the paint sample she'd taped to the wall yesterday. I'd grabbed a few extra gallons last night, just in case, so I got to work.

As I rolled the paint onto the walls, the room began to transform. The gentle lavender color gave the bakery an inviting feel. A couple of hours passed, and it was well into the evening when I slathered the last drop of paint onto the wall. I heard the kitchen door creak open, and Sugar emerged, looking a little frazzled but proud, a smudge of flour on her cheek.

Sugar burst out of the kitchen, practically bouncing, with a tray piled high with cookies—every kind imaginable. Chocolate chip, oatmeal raisin, snickerdoodles, and a few mystery flavors I couldn't even name.

"Try them." She beamed, shoving the tray toward me like it was the Holy Grail of baked goods.

Just as I reached for one, she froze, her eyes suddenly locking on the freshly painted walls. The tray wobbled in her hands, and with a clatter, she dropped it on the bar. Her mouth fell open before she slapped a hand over it dramatically.

"You painted this?" she gasped, still staring at the lilac walls. "The color I wanted? I thought you were still working on the electrical stuff."

I shrugged with a grin. "Figured I'd get a head start on it. Saw the paint sample and thought, why not?"

She blinked, still taking it all in. "It's perfect," she whispered, her eyes sparkling. "It's crazy to think that in less than a week, I'll be opening this place for business." She swept her gaze around the room. "Wow, I really need to figure out the seating and decorations."

I stepped closer, wrapping an arm around her waist and pulling her against me. "We can do it . . . together."

Her eyes lit up as she looked up at me. "Together?"

"Yes," I breathed. I grabbed a few of the cookies and shoved them into my lunchbox before turning back to her. With a grin, I asked her something that felt bold,but right. "Want to do something no one's ever done before? Have dinner . . . at my place?"

Sugar

"I think she's still staring at us," I said, peeking through the blinds of Willie's living room.

Sure enough, his neighbor was still watching us from across the street.

From the kitchen, Willie chuckled. "Oh, I'm sure she is. Small towns are like that—everyone's always in everyone's business."

"I don't know if I could ever get used to that," I admitted, letting the blinds fall back into place.

"You will . . . eventually," he said with a knowing smile.

I turned back around, still not convinced, but a little more amused by it all. Willie's house was a cozy, one-story brick home. The furniture was worn, with soft, faded cushions and a few nicks on the wooden coffee table, but it all added to the charm.

I wandered toward the back of the house, where the kitchen opened up on one side. The scent of garlic and simmering sauce filled the air, and I spotted Willie at the stove, stirring a pot of spaghetti.

I leaned against the doorway, watching him for a moment, then broke the comfortable silence. "Where's your bedroom?"

He glanced over his shoulder, a smirk tugging at his lips. "Down the hall, last door on the right. Why, thinking of checking it out?"

I laughed, but there was a playful glint in his eyes that made my heart skip. "Maybe . . . just curious."

He finished cooking, and we sat down at the wooden table to eat.

"You mentioned this was the first time anyone's ever come over?" I asked and twirled a forkful of pasta.

He nodded, looking a bit shy. "Yeah, not many women want to spend time with Wee Willie."

A tug at my heartstrings pulled me forward, and I reached across the table to take his hand. "I want to be with you, Willie. There's nothing wee about you."

He squeezed my hand in return. The moment felt heavy, but comforting, like we both finally understood each other in a way we hadn't before.

We lingered over dinner, our conversation flowing effortlessly as the evening stretched on. By the time we finished eating, the spaghetti was long gone, and the wine bottle was nearly empty. The light from the kitchen cast a warm glow over the table.

After we cleared the plates, Willie stood up and disappeared. Moments later, he returned, grinning as he set the plate of cookies in front of me.

"Ready for round two?"

I smiled, catching the playfulness in his eyes. "Alright, let's do this."

We started the taste test, going cookie by cookie, commenting on each one like professional critics. The clock on the wall ticked softly in the background, but time seemed irrelevant. Between the laughter and occasional cookie crumbs falling on the table, the hours melted away. By the time we were finished, the cookies were nearly gone, and the night had settled in fully, the kitchen now dimly lit by the soft moonlight streaming in from outside.

Willie leaned back in his chair, a contented smile on his face. "These were all amazing, Sugar."

I laughed, feeling a little glow of pride. "Maybe I could be a decent baker after all. Cookies are definitely my specialty."

Still smiling, he surveyed the plate of half-eaten treats. "The people of this town will be lined up down the block to get a taste of Sugar's cookies."

"Sugar's cookies," I repeated, meeting his eyes with a smile.

Underneath the table, our hands found each other, fingers intertwined, and we sat in that sweet, cozy silence for a while.

Willie grinned and grabbed the legs of my chair, pulling me closer until we were side by side. "You never did get to see that bedroom, did you?" he teased, his voice low and playful.

With a mischievous smile, I leaned in a little. "No, I didn't. And I think I'd like to continue the tour . . . There's one more cookie flavor you haven't sampled tonight."

He arched a brow, a sly smile curling his lips. "Is it the same one I got a taste of earlier this morning?" he asked, his tone dripping with suggestion.

I shrugged, pretending to be coy. "Maybe . . ."

We stumbled toward the bedroom, our feet awkwardly tangling together as we bumped into walls and nearly knocked over a lamp in the hallway. I ended up half draped over Willie as our mouths met in a clumsy, eager kiss. It was messy, passionate, and utterly uncoordinated.

"Wait," he murmured against my lips, pulling back just enough to break the kiss.

His eyes sparkled as he disappeared into the darkness of the hallway.

I stood there, confused and flushed, until he reappeared,

holding up a little apron. It was a soft pastel, and embroidered right on the pocket was the word *Sugar* in a looping script.

"My neighbor made it for you today," he said with a proud grin, running his hand over the apron like he was modeling it. "She was going to surprise you at the bakery's opening, but I've got a different idea."

I raised an eyebrow, trying not to laugh. "And what's that?"

His smile turned devilish. "I think I'd like you to take off your clothes and wear it for me right now."

I stared at him for a second, then burst into laughter. "You're serious?"

"As serious as an overbaked cookie." He winked, giving the apron a little twirl.

I shook my head, still laughing, but the heat between us hadn't gone anywhere. "Alright, apron boy," I teased, slowly peeling off my dress, "let's see how this works out."

With a playful shove, I sent Willie stumbling backward, landing awkwardly on the flannel bedspread. He looked up at me, wide-eyed, trying to play it cool, but his grin betrayed him.

I stepped out of my sundress, letting it fall dramatically to the floor. My perky cherries were fully on display, and my puffy floof was already glistening with excitement.

His eyes went wide, his mouth opening slightly as he took it all in, like a kid caught sneaking into the cookie jar.

Turning around with a cheeky little wiggle of my hips, I bent over just enough to give him a teasing view and held the apron strings behind me. "Well, come on," I said, barely holding back a grin. "Be a good boy and tie my apron, would you?"

Willie fumbled for the strings, hands shaky as he tried to keep up with my pace. I turned around in just a little apron covering my lower bits. "Do you like it?"

His eyes went wide, his mouth opening slightly as he took it all in. "You look . . . perfect."

I glanced down at the apron and back at him, and warmth spread over my cheeks. "Thank you. No one's ever done something this nice—taking care of me like this."

He smiled. "You deserve it, Sugar. And a whole lot more."

I got on top of him, and he held onto my waist as I wrapped my legs around him. "I am the boss in here."

"Yes, ma'am," he murmured as I rubbed my bare pussy along his jeans.

"First order of business?" I asked with a teasing lilt

"Tell me," he moaned, lips grazing my neck like he couldn't get enough.

"I need some milk for my dessert later."

I pushed him back, still straddling his waist, and then rose up on my knees just enough so my breasts hovered right in front of his face.

"Go on," I purred, grinning. "Be a good farmer and milk your cow."

He let out a low, appreciative "Mmm" as he eagerly complied, his mouth finding its target with enthusiasm.

Willie didn't hesitate, taking one of my nipples into his mouth and giving it a firm tug, like he was pulling on an udder. The sensation sent a jolt through me and I gasped. He alternated between sucking and gently pulling.

With a soft pop, he pulled away just long enough to look up at me. "Am I being a good farmer boy?"

"The best," I breathed, my voice thick with pleasure. "Now keep going."

He didn't need to be told twice. He brought his mouth back to my breasts, tugging and biting softly, each movement sending waves of heat through me. Sliding his hands up to cup my breasts, he kneaded them while working his mouth over my nipples. He tugged with his mouth again, his tongue teasing with just the right amount of pressure before biting down softly, making me arch closer to him.

"So much milk for your cookies later." I cried out, my orgasm building as I ground against his jeans.

"I need to taste your cookie," he pleaded, and I pulled away from him.

"Tsk, tsk." I clicked with my tongue. "Not this time, Willie. I want your Pressure Washer inside me tonight."

I lifted off him and pulled off his shirt and jeans.

"Are you sure?" He'd asked me this question earlier.

I grabbed his hands. "When will you realize that I am so attracted to you, Willie? I'm attracted to your body, to your mind and your selflessness. I've only known you for a couple days, but I know you're a special person."

He nodded. "Okay," he murmured and then shimmied out of his boxers.

I squealed in delight. "You let me be the boss tonight, Willie. You deserve it."

He tugged on my nipple again. "Yes, chef," he said after popping off me.

"Spread your legs, and let me play with you."

He let his knees go slack, and I kneeled in front of him, watching his flaccid Wiener flop forward. I reached up, and it was too small to fit in the entirety of my hand, so I used my index finger and thumb to coax it to life.

He moaned, and I tugged on it, playing with his sensitive skin on the underside of his shaft. "You like that?"

He moaned again. "I want you to smear your frosting on me. I wanna be a pie you can take with heavy, heavy cream on top. Okay?"

"Yes, chef."

I worked up and down his shaft, and he grew to life with the touch of my hands. Precum beaded in his slit, and I leaned down, licking it up.

"Careful, Sugar. You might get electrocuted with all the moisture."

I paused and looked up at him. "I love when you talk techy to me."

He chuckled, and I focused back on tugging him to life. "You're doing such a good job," I praised as he hardened beneath my fingers. "I'm going to need to add a little butter here, Willie."

He nodded, but said nothing as I leaned over and spat on his Juicy Dribbler. "Now, I have to mix it all up."

I used my fingers and rubbed up and down, tugging him forward and stretching him as far as I could.

"Fuck, I love Sugar's cookies."

"Yeah, you do." I scratched under his shaft with my long nails, and he twitched. "That feel good?"

"So g-good." His glasses were all fogged over.

I straightened and wrapped my legs around him. "I need to use my mixer now, Willie. I need to mix all that goodness up."

He furrowed his eyebrows, but once he understood, he closed his legs to allow me to mount him. With my plumpness, I had to spread my cheeks to settle over both of his legs. Slowly, I lowered myself down, and when I was perfectly aligned, I realized I had found my place. I slid right into Wee Willie.

I paused for a moment, letting the sensation wash over me. There was no pain, no stretching, no oversized Antenna trying to push too far. It fit perfectly, like a small pecker nestled snugly in a cave. It was exactly what I needed.

"You feel so good," I whispered as he gripped my thick hips and guided me, rocking me gently back and forth.

The movement was different from what I was used to—no aggressive thrusting like with the Titty Ticklers. This was slower, more intimate, with subtle motions of my hips, something I'd picked up from my online research. It felt right—no out-of-breath bouncing, just smooth, controlled movements. The Weedle was definitely a better fit for me.

I wrapped my arms around his neck, my stiff nipples grazing his cheek and making him shiver.

"It's time to mix all the flour up, Willie," I crooned as I started moving in slow, deliberate circles, like a mixer churning dough.

I threw in a few light thrusts, and he moaned, his breathing ragged.

He slid his fingers down, trying to find my floof, but I was pressed so close against him that he struggled. "Can I get on top so I can help you out, chef?"

I nodded, and with surprising ease, he grabbed my back and shifted us so he was on top. From this new angle, he spread my legs wide, and his fingers found my clit, expertly rubbing as he held my waist. My lips ground against him as he moved, his touch sending waves of pleasure through me.

His Hot Pocket thrust into me, and he groaned with every movement. The friction against my clit was exactly what I needed, inching me closer to the edge. Every thrust, every stroke of his fingers, had me teetering on the brink, ready to turn into a soggy biscuit.

His short, shallow thrusts created a gentle rhythm, making it feel like he was exploring every inch of me with care. There was something oddly satisfying in the way his smallness allowed for more focus on the sensations around us—his hand gripping my hips, his breath against my skin, the way his body moved with mine. It was intimate in a different way, more about the connection than any grand gestures.

Willie kept a steady rhythm with his fingers, teasing me with just the right pressure. The way he circled my clit, combined with the slow grind of his hips, sent me spiraling toward release. With one final stroke, the tension snapped, and I exploded. My orgasm crashed over me, leaving me trembling and clinging to him as the waves of pleasure washed through me.

"I'm going to frost your biscuit now. The final step," he groaned proudly.

"I want a cream pie, Willie. Cover my sweet treat with your hot, wet icing," I purred.

"I'm the farmer nooow!" Willie bellowed as his release came in a sudden burst, like a fire truck spraying its hose. He pulled out, gripping his still-throbbing shaft, and finished by coating my folds with his warm fluid. Once he was done, he leaned down and took my nipples into his mouth, sucking deeply before pulling away with a wink. "Can't wait until these udders produce real milk for an after-dessert drink."

Curious, I reached down and dipped my finger into the sopping mess he'd left on my skin, the warmth of his release spreading across me. I brought my finger to my lips and took a small lick, savoring the salty taste.

"Mmm," I hummed. "Tastes like I've got the perfect ingredient for some sticky buns."

"I think I'd sign up for that taste test any day." Willie laughed and rolled onto his side as he pulled me closer.

"With this kind of frosting, I could open a whole new section at the bakery. Specialty treats only."

He reached for my hand, his fingers tangling with mine, and we lay there for a few comfortable minutes. Eventually, he pulled me up, and we stumbled our way to the shower. The warm water poured over us. We laughed as we scrubbed each other clean, the air filled with steam and the kind of easy playfulness that felt like it could last forever.

When we finally crawled into bed, Willie wrapped an arm around me, pulling me close like I was some prized possession he wasn't letting go of anytime soon. His breathing slowed as he fell asleep, his body snug against mine, and I couldn't help but grin into the darkness.

As I lay there, watching the moonlight creep through the curtains, I knew moving to Rantucky had been the best decision I'd ever made. But meeting Willie? That's when my life truly flipped on its head—in the best, quirkiest way possible.

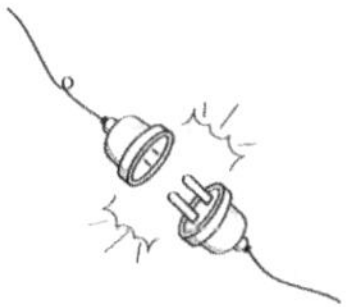

Willie

When I woke up the next morning, Sugar was gone from the house, but there was a small note on the bed next to me.

Willie,
Had a spark of creativity. Went to get an early start at the bakery. Meet me there when you wake.
XO Sugar

I dressed quickly and headed out the door, toolbox in hand. The quiet streets led me to Main Street, where I caught sight of her through the bakery's large front window. Inside, she was already busy rearranging furniture I recognized from the previous owners—worn but charming tables and chairs, perfectly suited to the cozy space she was crafting.

Pushing open the door, I was greeted by the comforting smell of freshly baked goods. She turned, beaming, her face lit up with pride.

"Hi," I said, walking up to her and pressing a quick kiss to her cheek.

She radiated happiness, her excitement almost contagious.

"Sit," she instructed, gesturing to one of the chairs in the corner.

I did as she asked, the chair familiar beneath me. She stood before me, practically bouncing on her feet, her eyes sparkling with joy.

"I did it," she exclaimed.

"Did what?" I asked, watching as she disappeared into the back, only to return moments later with a plate full of cookies.

She placed it carefully on the table between us and sat across from me.

My gaze shifted from the cookies to her. "Sugar," I said softly, "you didn't have to do this."

On the plate sat a dozen perfectly baked sugar cookies. She fidgeted slightly as she spoke. "I was so scared I'd jinx something if I tried this recipe. I was terrified that if I baked these, it would bring back memories of kids who used to call me the Sugar Cookie Killer or worse, I'd end up with the same fate as my parents."

She sighed deeply, and I reached out, intertwining our fingers together.

"It's been haunting me for so long, this fear of messing up, of history repeating itself. I didn't want to feel like a failure every time I looked at a batch of cookies. Today, I just felt like it was time. I had to face the creative block."

I squeezed her hand. "You did it," I said, giving her an encouraging smile. "And they look perfect."

She smiled back, her eyes shining with relief. "I finally feel like I've taken back something that used to hold me down. It's like I'm in control again, not the memories, not the fear."

I picked up one of the cookies and took a bite, letting the

sweetness melt in my mouth. "These are amazing," I said. "You've really done it, Sugar. You've overcome your past."

"I think I found what I'm going to specialize in."

I looked down at the plate, realizing how important this moment was for her. "Your parents would be so proud of you."

Sugar

I could hardly believe the bakery's opening day had finally arrived. I had poured my heart and soul into getting to this moment. Tammie was coming to town, and the only thing left to do was hang the sign Willie and I had hand painted.

Willie stood with the lilac and white sign in his hands, the colors perfectly complementing the bakery's cozy interior. The soft lavender background and crisp white lettering were the perfect representation of all the hard work and love we had put into this dream.

I watched as he carefully hung the sign above the entrance. It felt surreal, seeing it up there—*Sugar's Cookies*—the name gleaming proudly against the fresh paint.

"I can't believe it's finally happening," I murmured, more to myself than to him.

The opening day of the bakery had felt like an impossible dream for so long, something I had worked tirelessly for. Now, here it was, all laid out before me.

Willie glanced back at me with a proud smile, wiping his hands on his jeans as he admired the sign. "You made it happen," he said warmly. "This place is yours, Sugar."

I nodded, a mix of excitement and nerves bubbling inside me. "I really did," I whispered, letting the reality sink in.

Soon, the bakery would be filled with friends and customers.

"My parents would be proud," I said softly and interlocked my fingers with his.

Willie gave my hand a gentle squeeze and nodded toward the bakery. "Come on," he said with a smile. "Let's go make sure all the cookies are set."

We stepped inside, and the aroma of freshly baked cookies hit me. Rows of perfectly golden sugar cookies, chocolate chips, and snickerdoodles lined the counter, each one a little masterpiece. The cookies weren't just baked goods—they were pieces of me, bits of love and history rolled into dough.

"I guess I really did have the baking gene in me all along," I said. "It just needed a little coaxing to come out."

Willie grinned at me, raising an eyebrow. "Oh, I've always known you had something special in you. Just needed the right . . . touch."

I playfully swatted his arm. "Speaking of touch, don't think I've forgotten what's coming for you after this opening. I know pie's your favorite."

"Oh, I'm in for quite the treat."

I laughed. "You better believe it. You've seen how good I am with rolling dough—just wait 'til I'm rolling you later."

Willie's eyes gleamed with mischief. "I've seen how you knead too . . . and I'm more than ready for some of that action after we close up shop."

I smirked and bit my lip. "Trust me, by the end of tonight, I'll have you begging for seconds."

He pulled me close for a quick kiss. "Just don't wear me out too much. You know how hard it is to keep up with a master baker."

I winked.

Willie laughed, shaking his head as he looked around the bakery. "I'm . . . I'm really glad I met you, Sugar," he said. "Without you, I wouldn't be this confident in myself. I'd always be the guy people made fun of around town, the one no one took seriously. With you by my side, I feel like people are finally going to see me for who I really am. You make me feel like I'm enough, like I can be more than the jokes or pathetic looks. I'm more than the guy who will never get a girl because of his Slim Jim." He gave my hand a gentle squeeze, his eyes full of gratitude. "You changed all that for me."

I smiled at him, and warmth spread through my chest. "Thank you for being open with me, Willie. Without you, I wouldn't have discovered this part of myself. The cookies, the bakery, everything . . . it all feels like it was meant to be, but I wouldn't have found the courage without you believing in me."

I glanced over at the extra luxurious POS system he'd upgraded for me and couldn't help but grin as I pointed to it. "And I definitely wouldn't have the fanciest tech in the entire town without you."

Willie chuckled, wrapping his arm around me. "Anything for you, Sugar."

We stood together for a moment, just taking in the sight of the bakery.

"You know, I think you might've just made the best cookies in all of Rantucky."

I laughed and nudged him with my elbow. "You're just saying that because you want a taste of my secret batch."

"Well, you are the sweetest thing in here," he teased back, leaning in to kiss my cheek.

Willie glanced over toward the front door, and his face lit up. "Uh, Sugar? I think you've got company."

I turned to see Tammie banging on the glass with her fist, her face pressed up against the window. "Let me in. I need to see this masterpiece!" she hollered.

I hurried to the door and threw it open.

Tammie immediately engulfed me in her familiar, fierce hug. "Girl, you did it," she squealed, squeezing me tight before pulling back to give me a quick once-over. "You look amazing, and this place—"

Her jaw dropped as she stepped inside, spinning around to take it all in. The bakery was bathed in shades of soft lilac and creamy whites. Delicate lace curtains framed the windows, and plush, cushioned chairs were tucked around small round tables. Willie's neighbor had donated a few vintage pieces—an ornate mirror, a delicate China cabinet, and even a dainty chandelier that hung over the seating area, giving the space a bit of old-world charm. Behind the cash register hung an embroidered sign that read *Sugar's Cookies* in elegant, swirling letters, another gift from the same neighbor who had insisted on adding her personal touch.

"I can't believe it," Tammie breathed, spinning around one more time before her eyes landed on Willie. "You must be her boyfriend, Willie."

I blinked, taken aback. We hadn't exactly put a label on anything yet, but Willie, in true Willie fashion, didn't miss a beat. He walked right over, stuck out his hand, and gave her a firm shake.

"Yep, that's me. The luckiest boyfriend," he declared confidently.

Then, with a dramatic flourish, he ripped off his plain button-down shirt, revealing a ridiculous T-shirt underneath that said The Luckiest Boyfriend Ever, with a big, bold arrow pointing up toward his face.

My mouth went agape. "That has to be the kindest thing anyone has ever done for me."

Tammie burst into laughter, clutching her sides. "Oh my God, you two are perfect," she managed between giggles.

"Should we open the bakery for business?" Willie looked outside the door, and I couldn't believe what I saw.

I nodded. "Let's open for business."

I stood at the door, peeking out the window in disbelief, my heart swelling with excitement. The entire town had shown up, eager to see the bakery we'd poured so much love into. The moment I pushed the door open and walked outside to announce the bakery was officially opened for business, everyone cheered.

Willie jumped right into action, charming everyone as he grabbed cookies from the display case, making sure each one was carefully placed in the little bakery bags we'd decorated with lavender ribbons. He moved with an energy I hadn't seen before, laughing and joking with customers, even tossing in the occasional extra cookie "on the house," just to see people smile.

Meanwhile, Tammie stood at the door like a bubbly hostess, greeting everyone with her signature warmth. "Welcome to Sugar's Cookies! Come on in and try the best cookies in town!" she'd say, practically bouncing on her toes.

Every time she announced it, Willie and I shared the same mischievous look and chuckle.

I stayed behind the counter, my hands working nonstop as I bagged up cookies, carefully placing each order together. The line seemed endless, but I didn't mind; I was too caught up in the magic of it all. People kept complimenting the decor, saying how cozy and welcoming it felt. This was what I'd always dreamed of.

As the hours passed, the line slowly dwindled until, finally, the last customer walked out the door with a bag of snickerdoodles, waving as they left. The three of us stood in the empty bakery, a bit breathless but beaming from ear to ear.

Tammie walked over to me, her eyes shining with pride. She pulled me into a tight hug, and I could feel her smile against my shoulder. "You did it, Sugar. You really did it. Your parents would be so proud. You're living out their legacy."

Tears pricked at my eyes as I hugged her back, the weight of her words sinking in. "Thank you," I whispered. "I couldn't have done it without you . . . or without Willie."

Willie, hearing his name, looked up from where he'd been wiping down the counter and grinned.

I looked around the bakery—the flour-dusted countertops, the half-empty cookie trays, the embroidered sign hanging proudly on the wall—and knew Tammie was right. My parents would have been proud.

Tammie glanced at her phone and sighed. "Alright, I've got to head out," she said, pulling me into a final hug. "But I'll be back to check in on you, promise."

"You better," I teased, squeezing her back. "It wouldn't be the same without you."

She gave Willie a playful punch on the arm. "Take care of her, okay?"

"You know I will," he replied with a smile.

We walked her to the door and watched as she waved and disappeared down the street. The bakery fell quiet again, and as Willie turned back to me, we stood in the stillness, just the two of us.

"Well," he chuckled, "looks like we survived."

"Barely," I laughed, "I was half expecting you to short-circuit halfway through the day."

He smirked. "Please, if I can handle wiring this whole place without frying myself, I can handle a crowd of cookie fanatics. But you? I was sure you'd crumble."

"Well, I do like to keep things sweet," I shot back, raising an eyebrow.

Willie grabbed the last sugar cookie from the container and

snapped it in half for us. "To the baker and the electrician," he declared, holding up his half.

"To cookies."

We clinked our cookie halves together like we were celebrating with champagne.

He took a bite and groaned like he'd just tasted pure heaven. "Yep, cookies are definitely your calling."

I giggled. "Well, the only pies I'll be baking for you now are cream pies."

The corner of his lips twisted into a mischievous smirk.

"Straight from the dairy farm."

Epilogue

WILLIE

My pregnant wife was sprawled out on the bed, and I was ready to plug in like an over-amped cord finally finding its socket.

"If you're tasting my sweetness tonight, just know I'm so big, you might forget I'm even here," she teased, her round belly between us.

I laughed, giving her tummy a little rub before sliding down to the bushy forest beneath. I was on a mission tonight, and her warm nest was my destination.

"I figured it was about time you got a little treat after running around all day."

We'd opened the bakery nine months ago, and just a week after our grand opening, Sugar found out she was baking more than just cookies—she was pregnant. Best news we'd ever gotten. She moved in, and from that moment on, we'd been stuck together like frosting on a cinnamon roll.

Her cookies had become the talk of the town; people were lining up from the big city just to snag a taste. But little did they know, every night I got the sweetest dessert on the menu—straight from the source.

I settled between her thighs with a grin. Her scent hit me first, warm and sweet, and I licked my lips. I started slowly, giving her a soft, teasing lick just to hear that little gasp she always made.

"Does it count as a cream pie if I'm already pregnant?" Her hips bucked against my face.

"Absolutely. You know I love when you save that treat for me," I murmured against her, letting my breath tickle her clit before working her with my mouth again.

I took my time and alternated between gentle licks and firmer sucks.

"You're my favorite dessert," I muttered with a chuckle, nibbling her clit just to hear her gasp again.

Her fingers tightened in my hair. If this was the kind of dessert I got to taste every night, I'd gladly be her taste tester for life.

"Willie." She mewled. "Put your Biscuit Brisket inside me."

"Come on then." I patted the side of the bed.

Sugar shimmied off, as quickly as her round belly allowed, and hopped down from the bed. She turned around and rested her forearms on the bed.

"I love seeing you like this," I murmured, running my hand down the curve of her back.

Ever since she'd gotten pregnant, we'd taken our cow and farmer roleplay to a whole new level, and I wasn't complaining.

"Go on, let me feel that Willie, Willie," she giggled.

"Don't you worry, darling. It's coming," I chuckled, stripping off my pants in one smooth motion.

I didn't need to ask anymore if I was enough for her. She made me feel it every single day, in the way she looked at me, laughed with me, and trusted me with all her sweetness. And tonight, I was going to make sure she felt every bit of how much she meant to me.

I pushed inside her, but in this position, if I thrust too

much, I'd pop off, so I kept one hand held tightly onto the meaty flesh above her hips. With my free hand, I reached around and grabbed her nipples, pulling them toward the ground.

"Getting myself ready for the farm. I need to get enough milk for the pies tonight," I moaned while slamming into her.

"I'm ready to be milked."

Sugar's nipples were always a little large, but since she'd gotten pregnant, they were the same size as my Short Fishing Pole. My hand drifted down her belly as I pumped in quick, eager thrusts against her hips.

"Oh my God, I'm gonna come," she gasped.

Sugar usually needed a little extra love down below, but one of the best things about her being pregnant was that the slightest touch had her seeing stars.

"I swear, I'm keeping you pregnant forever, Sugar," I murmured.

I leaned in, giving her hardened nipples one more teasing tug, and suddenly felt a warm spray hit my hand.

"What the—?" I yelped, completely caught off guard.

"Oh my gosh," Sugar gasped, eyes wide. "I'm leaking."

"Is that . . . is that bad?" I stammered, panicking that I might've done something to hurt the baby.

She shook her head with a reassuring smile. "No, it's normal. My doctor mentioned it could happen."

Curious, I lifted my hand to my mouth and tasted the sweet milk. "Whoa, this is actually delicious. Your body's got a knack for making good stuff."

She laughed. "After you're a good boy and finish me off, I'll let you have a real taste of milk."

My breath hitched—Sugar always knew how to keep me on my toes.

"In fact," she said, pulling away and meeting my eyes with a mischievous glint, "why don't you sit on the bed? I'll get you to the finish line while you milk me."

"Are you sure?" My pulse quickened.

"Absolutely." She grinned. "They say orgasms help induce labor, and I'm already a week overdue. So really, you're just doing me a favor."

I repositioned myself, scooting back until I was sitting against the headboard. I spread my thighs wide for her to sit. Sugar climbed over me, her round belly creating just enough distance that she had to stretch out a bit to reach my Member. Her eyes sparkled with that familiar glint as she wrapped her hand around me, using her thumb to tease.

The pressure from her thumb, moving in slow, deliberate circles, sent a deep shiver through me. Being on the smaller side made it even more intense—every tiny movement heightened the sensation.

"Come on, Farmer. My milk needs to come out."

I slowly lifted my hands to her breasts, giving her nipples a gentle pull, tugging them forward.

"That's it," she whimpered, grinding her hips against my thigh.

Her movements grew more intense, drawing me fully to life.

When I gave her left nipple another firm tug, a sudden stream of milk shot out, spraying my glasses. I wiped the milk off, but I wanted more of where that had come from. Intrigued, I repeated the motion on her right breast, and soon enough, both were squirting out in rhythm. Without thinking, I opened my mouth wide, eager to catch every drop.

"That's it. Taste me. Lick me up." She tugged on me harder, pulling me forward with such intensity.

Her hips bucked wildly, moving with a desperate rhythm as she edged closer to her climax.

"Taste my after-dessert drink," she demanded breathlessly, her body trembling, on the verge of letting go.

I inched closer until my lips were barely brushing against her skin. Gently, I cupped her breasts in my hands, marveling at their fullness, the way they felt so soft, yet heavy against my palms. Her breath hitched as I brought my mouth to her nipple, teasing it first with my tongue, tasting the saltiness of her skin. With a slow, deliberate pull, I latched on, drawing her deeper into my mouth.

The first stream of milk hit my tongue, warm and sweet, and I moaned against her, surprised by how thick and rich it was. I sucked harder, greedily, letting the milk fill my mouth until I could taste nothing else, feeling it slide down my throat as I swallowed. It wasn't just the flavor—it was the way it seemed to coat every part of me.

I moved my hand to her other breast, squeezing harder this time, coaxing more of that warm, rich liquid to flow. I alternated between her nipples, taking my time with each one, pulling and sucking until they were slick with my saliva, her long, pointed tips swelling in response.

She tangled her fingers in my hair, pulling me closer.

I drank from her with a hunger that bordered on desperation, as if her sweetness was the only thing that could quench the fire burning inside me. Her milk spilled over my lips, dribbling down my chin as I latched on harder, sucking and pulling until her nipple throbbed against my tongue. I savored every thick, creamy drop as her taste filled my mouth, warm and rich, until I couldn't tell where she ended and I began.

Her breath stuttered with each tug, her hips rocking toward me, desperate for more as I milked her with greedy, relentless pulls. Her body trembled, giving in to me completely, and I tightened my grip, drawing even deeper, determined to take everything she had to offer. The more I drank, the more I craved, lost in the way her warmth flowed into me, drop by sinful drop, until I was drowning in her, addicted to the way she surrendered, the way she let me take her.

"You're making quite the mess."

I grinned and wiped my mouth with the back of my hand. "What can I say? You're my personal drink. And I've gotta admit, you're sweeter than any dessert I've ever had."

She snorted, rolling her eyes. "Now, are you gonna finish your 'drink,' or do I need to show you how it's done?"

I couldn't help but laugh. "Oh, I'm just getting started, Sugar."

I dove back in, my hands working over her breasts as I latched onto her nipple, sucking hard. The warm, sweet milk poured out, drenching my tongue and dripping down my chin. I let out a muffled laugh against her skin. I was like someone devouring the last bit of ice cream straight from the carton, and I was determined to get every last drop. My fingers kneaded and squeezed, milking her with a kind of urgency that had her whimpering, her body jerking each time my mouth pulled at her.

Meanwhile, she worked me with her fingers. She didn't try to grab me with her whole hand—she knew that wouldn't work—but instead teased me with just her fingertips, those little flicks and tugs that made my eyes roll back.

"You're gonna make me lose it," I groaned.

Then, out of nowhere, she let out a scream, her whole body seizing up as she came, trembling and breathless. That was it—I couldn't hold back anymore. I came hard, all over her hand.

Just when I thought it was over, she shot another stream of milk, splattering it all over my face.

I pulled back, gasping, absolutely drenched. "Are you trying to turn me into a milkshake?" I joked. I took off my glasses and wiped my eyes.

"Well, you did say you liked sweet things," she shot back, grinning down at me. "Looks like you're getting exactly what you asked for."

She leaned in, her tongue flicking over my cheek to catch a stray drop of milk. "You missed a spot," she murmured.

I pulled her in, and our lips crashed together as we tangled, our milk-slicked bodies pressing closer, sticky warmth binding us. She slid her fingers up my back, nails teasing, every touch electric and raw. The intensity swallowed us whole, and I never wanted to let go, lost in her heat, completely consumed by the way we moved together.

"Look at us," she said as she traced lazy patterns on my chest. "We're like a walking dessert bar."

"Hey, you're the one serving all the milk," I teased. "I'm just here to do the taste testing."

She rolled her eyes, but her smile didn't fade. Instead, she clung to me a little tighter, nestling into my arms as the last of our laughter faded into a comfortable silence. I pressed a kiss to her forehead.

Suddenly, she tensed up, her hands instinctively flying to her belly. Her eyes went wide, and for a second, I thought I might've done something wrong.

"Are you okay?" I asked, my heart skipping a beat.

She took a deep breath, her lips curling into a sly smile as she nodded. "I think . . . maybe that did work," she murmured, giving her belly a little pat. "Could be that all this, uh, exercise finally got things moving."

I stared at her, dumbfounded, before bursting into a fit of laughter. "You mean to tell me this whole time, I was just helping induce labor?"

I couldn't help but think about how I'd never seen myself as someone with a taste for the sweeter things in life. I'd always been the type who thought he preferred the rougher edges, something a little more bitter. But then came Sugar, turning everything upside down, showing me that sometimes, a bit of sweetness was exactly what I'd been missing all along.

She snorted, leaning in close. "If I end up going into labor, at least we'll know you've got the power to flip my switch."

"Well, they did say Milk and Cookies went together."

74

Acknowledgments

I'll keep this short and sweet—just like Willie.

To my alpha and beta team: thank you for the BEST comments. Madison, Madison, Julia, Michelle, Sammi, Nay-Nay, Jewel, Jordan, Sandra, Adrianna, Amy, and Amanda—thank you for trusting me with this cringe-worthy project and making it better.

To my editor, Jeanie: thank you for bringing Willie and Sugar to life with your magic.

Celena, as always, thank you for the laughs and your keen eye during the proofread.

And to Allyson with The Sparrow Collective: your first cover, and you KNOCKED it out of the park with the graphics and design. I couldn't be happier.

To my husband: you've never read one of my books in its entirety... until *Sugar's Cookies.* Thank you for coming home every night and asking me to read another chapter because it made you laugh. That meant the world to me.

Lastly, thank you. Writing sad stuff all the time can take a toll, and I needed to write this one mostly for myself. Knowing you've read it, enjoyed it, and shared it with your friends and family has been the sweetest gift.

Also by Vee Taylor

The Marchetti Men

A completed interconnected Mafia Series

One Chance

Second Guess

Third Degree

Fourth Wall

The University of Isles

A completed Romeo & Juliet inspired dark college romance

Into the Darkness

Into the Light

Between Dusk and Dawn

Chicago Raven's Hockey

Your Pucking Mom

About the Author

Vee Taylor is a passionate writer based in the suburbs outside of Chicago. With a lovingly supportive husband, two dogs, and two children, she finds inspiration from her mental health background and uses it to fuel her writing. Her passion for reading and writing began ten years ago, and she hasn't looked back since.

As an avid book lover, Vee is obsessed with all things bookish. She loves exploring new worlds, discovering new characters, and delving into different genres. Her favorite genres include dark romance, romantasy, and everything in between. When she's not writing, she can often be found with her nose buried in a book or scrolling aimlessly on social media.

Vee Taylor is so excited that you are here on this journey with her.

www.veetaylorauthor.com

www.ingramcontent.com/pod-product-compliance
Lightning Source LLC
Chambersburg PA
CBHW061705130726
47996CB00006B/2175